Ghouls Rule

The Ghosts of CREAKIE HALL in Ghouls Rule

Karen Wallace
and Tony Ross

Catnip

CATNIP BOOKS
Published by Catnip Publishing Ltd
14 Greville Street
London EC1N 8SB

This edition first published 2011

First published by Hamish Hamilton Ltd 1996
1 3 5 7 9 10 8 6 4 2

A CIP catalogue record for this book is available from
the British Library.

ISBN 978 1 846470 974

Printed in Poland

www.catnippublishing.co.uk

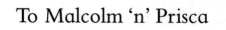

To Malcolm 'n' Prisca

CHAPTER 1

MIASMA BOGEY-MANDEVILLE sat by her attic window at the front of Creakie Hall and stared down at her favourite view. The thick black water of Bullfrog Lake shone dully in the sun. The high green hedges of the maze twisted and turned in a crazy pattern. Even after hundreds of years, it still made Miasma dizzy to look at it. And as for trying to find a way out of it, she chuckled at the memories of panic-stricken voices, pledging everything just to escape. It was more of a prison than a maze, really.

Miasma leaned back on her chair and sighed happily. Nothing had changed for hundreds of years.

Nor for that matter had Miasma. Her knee-length orange hair still shone like a stream of molten lava. Her green eyes still glittered like a cat's. And her face was still the ghostly silver of a single cloud on a moonlit night.

Far below Osbert Codseye, the gardener, was mowing the lawn. Osbert Codseye loved mowing the lawn. He rode his machine like a mediaeval knight riding his horse in procession. The stripes that emerged from behind him were velvety green and perfectly straight.

Watching Osbert Codseye mow the lawn usually had a hypnotic effect on Miasma. Usually, it was peaceful, reassuring and soothing.

But not that day. Miasma pulled a face and threw back her mane of orange hair. Ever since the time she had ventured below, things hadn't been the same. It had been exciting helping save Creakie Hall. Without her, Creakie Hall would have fallen down and the flesh'n'bloods would have had to sell up. It made Miasma proud to remember how everyone had worked together. She sighed. It had also been good to feel part of a family again.

She drummed her fingers on the arm of her heavy oak chair. Even though she had been happy to return to her life in the attic, now that seemed a long time ago.

Too long. The truth was Miasma Bogey-Mandeville was bored.

She let her eyes wander over to the edge of Bullfrog Lake. A man and woman were looking up at Creakie Hall and then staring down at a large piece of paper they held in their hands. Miasma raised her high curved eyebrows.

They were a strange-looking pair. Not the usual type of guest that visited Creakie Hall. They were wearing matching black and purple clothes. He had a shiny black suit with a purple shirt and purple shoes. She was squeezed into a tight purple dress with a wide black belt and high-heeled black shoes. Her stiff black hair was piled high above her head and in her right hand she held a slim black box with numbers on the front.

Miasma watched as the woman punched in a long series of numbers and nodded in the direction of Creakie Hall. Her fingers were stubby and they ended in ridiculously long painted red fingernails.

The man had a sharp face that was shiny with sweat. From time to time, he looked down at a large black suitcase by his feet.

The more Miasma watched them, the less she liked the look of them.

Something moved at her feet. Miasma looked down at the curly black-haired head of her husband Marmaduke. He was dressed in his favourite green and gold doublet and a silver-handled sword hung from his waist. It clanked as he crawled around the floor on his hands and knees. Miasma rolled her eyes. Marmaduke was building a cardhouse. It was more of a palace than a house. In fact it looked like Hampton Court.

Miasma glared at the towers and turrets, tenderly balanced on top of each other. She curled her lip. It might be a work of art but as far as she was concerned it was also a waste of time. Worse than that, Marmaduke had hardly spoken to her since he started building it.

Miasma's eyes wandered back to the lake. Now the two people were looking at Creakie Hall through binoculars. Her curiosity boiled over. An idea floated into her mind.

'Marmaduke,' she said sweetly. 'I'm going to do something completely outrageous.'

'That's nice, spookypet,' replied Marmaduke, his eyes fixed firmly on the seventh floor of his new tower.

'Marmaduke,' said Miasma, again. 'I'm going to turn myself into a huge black bullfrog. Then I'm going to fly out the window, dive into the lake and spy on two peculiar-looking people.'

'That's nice, ghostykins,' replied Marmaduke, carefully levering a King of Clubs into position.

'Marmaduke,' said Miasma, softly. 'Before I go, I'm going to jump on top of your stupid, boring cardcastle.'

'That's nice, bogeybaby,' replied Marmaduke, crawling across the floor to pick up another card.

That did it! Miasma's eyes sparkled

with fury. If there was one thing she really hated, it was being called bogeybaby!

Splat! A huge black bullfrog with bright green eyes jumped into the middle of the cardcastle and scattered cards all over the room. Then it jumped out of the window, sailed through the summer air and passed low across the lawn.

Osbert Codseye felt a rush of cold air by his left ear. He looked up and saw something truly horrible flying past him. It looked like a monstrous bullfrog. What's more, it was making a gleeful croaking sound.

Aaargh! His eyes rolled back in his head. But Osbert Codseye was made of tough stuff. He didn't fall off his lawnmower. The only problem was the straight velvety-green line. It wasn't straight any more. In fact it became wigglier and wigglier as the lawnmower drove itself round in circles. Finally it plunged into a flower bed and stopped in the middle of an enormous rose bush.

Plop! Miasma landed in the lake. The soupy black water felt delicious and soothing. She looked up at the attic window. It was so hot up there, so boring. Swimming in the lake was much more fun.

I should do this more often, she told herself. Then she kicked her webbed feet and hid under a lily pad just in front of the two peculiar-looking people standing on the bank.

CHAPTER 2

'WHADDYATHINK?' SAID ROGER Clawback in a low voice. His face had the hard, determined look of a questing weasel. Nothing was going to get in his way. 'I'm sure the old bat that owns it believed everything we said.'

For a second Miasma wondered whether calling someone a bat might be a compliment. She knew lots of bats and most of them were very nice.

'The old ones are the stupid ones,' sneered Ritzi Clawback. 'Especially ones with a name like that. I mean,

Gardenia Bogey-Mandeville. Sounds like a perfume for sewer rats.'

'Never mind her stupid name,' said Roger. 'Whaddyathink of the dump?'

'It'll do,' said Ritzi. She shrugged. 'We con the old bat out of her savings. We buy it cheap. We sell it pricey.'

'So let's get on with it,' replied Roger. He threw a half-chewed cigar into the lake and sniffed. 'You know, someone should fill in this water hole.'

'Yeah,' agreed Ritzi. 'It stinks of plants and animals.'

Miasma's bullfrog cheeks puffed up with rage. She jumped onto the lily pad and glared at the black and purple figures now walking up to the house. No one was ever going to fill in her precious Bullfrog Lake. Who were these disgusting creatures?

And what were they up to? Whatever it was, they must be stopped. But how? She needed to talk to Marmaduke immediately. Then Miasma remembered the cards scattered all over the floor of their attic room. Marmaduke might not be speaking to her.

In fact Marmaduke might be rather cross with her.

At that moment a terrible thing happened. A huge heron flew down to the side of the lake. It had curly black head feathers and a sword round its middle. It had a look in its eye of someone whose cardcastle had been jumped on and scattered all over the floor. It grabbed one of Miasma's back legs and yanked her out of the lake.

Suddenly Miasma found herself hanging upside down by one slippery back leg. Creakie Hall swung crazily two hundred feet below her.

'Say you're sorry,' muttered Marmaduke through his clenched beak. 'Say you're sorry for wrecking Hampton Court.'

'I'm sorry,' shouted Miasma. 'Marmaduke, something dreadful is going on. Two horrible people are trying to trick Gardenia into giving them all her money. Then they're going to buy Creakie Hall.' She began to howl. 'Then they're going to sell it!'

'What?' shouted Marmaduke. This time he completely forgot to keep his beak shut.

Miasma's slippery back leg dropped out.

Cold air rushed past Miasma's ears. As she fell, pictures of her life flashed past her eyes. And since Miasma had been around for so many years, there were a lot of pictures.

Suddenly the wiggly green stripes of the lawn rose up in front of her. Miasma was only a few feet from the ground when a miraculous thought occurred to her. She remembered that she could fly perfectly well on her own.

Whoosh! She roared back into the sky like a jetplane at an air display.

Deep inside the rosebush Osbert Codseye opened one battered eye. Above him he saw a heron with curly black head feathers and a sword tied around its middle. He blinked and looked again. Flying beside the heron was a huge black frog. The bullfrog was croaking and the heron was squawking. It sounded as if they were *talking* to each other. Then they looped the loop and disappeared *through* the attic window.

Osbert Codseye groaned. His eyes rolled back and he fell into the rosebush, clutching his head with both hands.

CHAPTER 3

AUNT GARDENIA BOGEY-MANDEVILLE sat cross-legged in the middle of the dining-room table, knitting a black and purple scarf.

Aunt Gardenia's passion was knitting. Everything in Creakie Hall had a knitted cover. Even Osbert Codseye's lawnmower. Aunt Gardenia had her best ideas when she knitted. It was only because she had been using up some old gold wool that she had thought of turning Creakie Hall into a hotel in the first place. Gold reminded her of little gold chairs.

And little gold chairs reminded her of hotel entrances. And hotel entrances reminded her of piles of peppermints wrapped in gold paper, sitting on a table by the front door.

Aunt Gardenia liked peppermints. And that was that. She had knitted a banner with *CREAKIE HALL HOTEL* picked out in gold. And since then everything had worked out wonderfully. Now Aunt Gardenia was knitting because she was thinking about her new guests, Ritzi and Roger Clawback. They seemed so interested in Creakie Hall. They wanted to make it even nicer than it already was, so that guests would love it even more than they already did. *Clack, clack, clack* went her knitting needles. And that was the most important thing of all to Aunt Gardenia. So she had decided it would be a good idea to do business with such a delightful young couple.

On the sofa opposite the dining-room table sat Polly and George Bogey-Mandeville, Aunt Gardenia's niece and nephew. They were staring at a black and purple card and they didn't look very happy. It said:

Roger and Ritzi Clawback.
Dreamland Developments
Doing the Best for Us. You

Except the '**Us**' was crossed out and '**You**' was written instead.

Polly looked up. The black and purple scarf already went twice around the room. It was a sure sign that Aunt Gardenia was thinking seriously about **Dreamland Developments**.

'It's quite simple, dears,' said Aunt Gardenia. *Clack, clack, clack* went the needles. 'First I give Ritzi and Roger all my savings for the hotel. Then they have promised to put in twice as much as me. Then we can afford to buy lots of lovely things for Creakie Hall so that everyone who comes

will love it more than ever.' She beamed and held up the long narrow scarf. 'They seem *such* nice people and they absolutely *adore* Creakie Hall.'

'But Creakie Hall is lovely as it is,' said George. 'People like it being old-fashioned.'

'And they love its knitted covers,' added Polly. 'Even the one on the chandelier.'

'Of course they do, dear,' said Aunt Gardenia, sweetly. 'But sometimes I think we should try and keep up with the times. A golf course perhaps, or a swimming pool.'

'A *swimming pool*?' cried Polly in a horrified voice. 'But there's Bullfrog Lake.'

'And Osbert hates swimming pools,' said George. 'They're noisy and smell of suntan lotion.'

'Osbert Codseye hates swimming pools because he can't swim,' said Aunt Gardenia firmly.

Polly looked once more at the black and purple card she was holding. 'Aunt Gardenia,' she said slowly. 'If you give these people all your money, what happens if they –'

At that moment, a bird in a knitted cover popped out of a clock and made a muffled cuckoo noise.

'Goodness me!' said Aunt Gardenia, putting down her needles. It was a sign that the meeting was over. 'Is that the time? The Milkwarm family will be here any minute.'

Polly and George looked at each other in dismay. Aunt Gardenia could be very stubborn, especially when she believed she was doing the right thing.

Outside a car crunched across the gravel.

'Here they are!' cried Aunt Gardenia. 'Children, check the best room is ready for them. Mrs Milkwarm said it was their first holiday for years and she sounded worn out, poor thing.'

Polly and George ran up the stairs to the first floor. The best room had a four-poster bed and its own balcony. Polly pulled open the door and

looked inside. There was a vase of flowers on the table and a brand-new knitted bedspread. It all looked lovely and inviting.

Outside the window, car doors slammed. Polly went out onto the balcony to shout a welcome but her voice died in her throat.

'What a dump,' said a pasty-faced boy, climbing out of the car. He had crew-cut blond hair and a T-shirt with *KIDS FIRST* written across it. 'There ain't even a swimming pool.'

'I ain't staying in a hotel with no swimming pool,' screamed a girl with hair like rats' tails and chocolate smeared all over her mouth.

A pale, thin woman climbed out of the car.

'There's a lovely lake in the grounds, darlings,' she said in a hopeless, pleading sort of way.

That must be Mrs Milkwarm, thought Polly. *No wonder she's tired and worn out.*

'Great,' muttered her son who was called Bruce. 'You can go jump in it.'

'And there's a fantastic maze,' added a low, patient voice.

Polly saw the stooped, balding figure of a man pulling heavy suitcases out of the back of the car.

That must be Mr Milkwarm, she thought.

'Terrific,' sneered his daughter, who was called Taffeta. 'You can get lost for a change.' She turned and prodded her brother. 'Hey! Who's that old crone with the knitting basket?'

Polly gasped and shut the window. She didn't want to hear any more.

'Polly!' It was George's voice. 'Come here quickly!'

Polly rushed out of the room to see

George standing at the end of the corridor. He was looking up at the flight of stairs in front of him.

George put his fingers to his lips and beckoned Polly to hurry.

Two seconds later Polly found herself staring face to face with the weirdest-looking cat. Its fur shone a ghostly silver. Its eyes were turquoise and they glowed like exploding stars.

'It's Cromwell,' whispered George.

Cromwell fixed them with his crazy eyes. Then he did two back flips, twirled like a top and pointed like a gun dog towards the attic.

'I think Cromwell's trying to tell us something,' whispered Polly.

George and Polly ran up two more flights of stairs to the attic floor. Then they turned right and went along the corridor until they came to a dead-end wall.

'That's funny,' said George in a puzzled voice. He felt along the wall.

'Something's different. I could have sworn –'

'Variety's the spice of life, flesh'n' bloods!' cried a voice above them.

A woman's face looked down. She had green eyes and long orange hair. She grinned a wolfish grin. As she spoke, a rope ladder uncoiled itself like a cobra and hung in the air.

Polly and George climbed up the ladder as fast as they could.

A moment later they stood in the oak-panelled room they remembered so well.

'Hello,' said Polly and George, shyly. Then they shook hands with the two people whose portraits hung in the front hall – their ancestors, Miasma and Marmaduke Bogey-Mandeville.

CHAPTER 4

THE STRANGE THING was that after the first 'hello', Polly and George couldn't think of anything to say. Even though they had all had such fun working together to make Creakie Hall into a hotel, the truth is that picking up where you left off with a pair of ghosts is rather an awkward thing to do.

Polly stared at her feet and blushed. And that's when she noticed the floor was covered in cards.

She said the first thing that came into her head. 'Have you been building a cardcastle?'

'No,' said Marmaduke.

'Yes,' said Miasma.

It was a bad start. They all stared at each other again. Then Miasma remembered an article she had read in a woman's magazine the last time she had ventured downstairs.

'My, how you've grown!' she cried, clasping her hands in front of her and beaming like a lighthouse. 'Who would have thought it? Why it only seems –'

'Cut the chat, spookypet,' said Marmaduke, briskly. Marmaduke had listened to a lot of bad gangster movies when he had ventured downstairs. 'We gotta get serious. This is an emergency.'

'Like you're still in the bath when the guests arrive for dinner,' crowed Miasma, remembering another article in her magazine.

Polly looked at George and rolled her eyes. 'If you're talking about those children,' she began. 'I know their manners –'

'I am *not* talking about those *disgusting* children,' cried Miasma. 'Although I have a few plans for them. I am talking about those *disgusting* adults who are trying to trick Aunt Gardenia into selling Creakie Hall.'

'Which disgusting adults?' said George.

'I don't know their names,' said Miasma. 'All I know is that they dress in purple and black and the woman looks like a great big cockroach.'

'Boiling oil, too good for them,' muttered Marmaduke, flicking over the pages of his *Terrible Tortures* book.

'They should be hanged, drawn, and quart –'

'Marmaduke!' cried Polly. 'Put that book away!'

'That's right!' cried Miasma. 'You have to think modern, ghostykins. We should zap them with a laser gun.'

'You'll do no such thing,' said Polly firmly.

She remembered only too well the last time Marmaduke and Miasma had decided to help out downstairs. Pretty soon, Polly and George had needed all the help they could get just to get things back to normal.

'I think you had better tell us exactly what you know,' said George in his deepest voice. He looked at Polly. He knew she was thinking about the business card they had seen in Aunt Gardenia's dining room and wondering if there was any connection with the two people dressed in black and purple.

So Miasma repeated word for word what she had overheard as she hid under the lily pad in the soupy water of Bullfrog Lake.

When she had finished, Polly and George looked at each other again. Things were even more serious than they thought.

'Their names are Ritzi and Roger Clawback,' said Polly, slowly. Then they told Marmaduke and Miasma about the black and purple business card.

'Huh,' cried Miasma, throwing back her mane of orange hair. 'We'll sort out those thieving knaves, won't we, ghostykins? By the time we're finished with them, they'll, they'll –'

George held up his hand. 'Wait a minute,' he said. 'Before we do anything, we have to have proof.

Aunt Gardenia trusts them and you know what she's like once her mind is made up.'

'He's right,' said Polly. 'That black and purple scarf she's knitting already goes twice around the dining room.'

George nodded. 'We have a big problem,' he said.

'Yippee!' cried Miasma. She threw up her arms and capered across the room. 'It'll be just like old times!'

'Wait a minute,' said George again. 'We have to get a few things straight.'

'Of course you do,' agreed Miasma.

'Definitely no appearing and disappearing,' said George. Out of the corner of his eye, he saw Osbert Codseye zigzagging across the lawn towards the front hall. 'Some people find it upsetting.'

'Of course they do,' agreed Marmaduke.

'And no boiling oil, hanging, drawing or quartering,' said Polly.

'How about a blow with a sharp instrument?' suggested Marmaduke, making chopping movements with his hands.

'No axes,' said Polly firmly.

'We agree to everything,' cried Miasma. 'Don't we, spookypet? We'll start immediately!'

And before either Polly or George could reply, Miasma and Marmaduke had disappeared.

'Oops,' said Miasma's voice somewhere near the ceiling. 'That's what you did last time.'

'You did it first.'

'Didn't.'

'Did.'

'*Didn't.*'

Then both voices faded away.

'Polly! George!' It was Aunt

Gardenia. 'Where are you? I have a surprise for you.'

A fireman's pole appeared in front of them.

'Come on,' cried George, sliding all the way down to the first floor. 'There's no time to lose!'

CHAPTER 5

POLLY AND GEORGE were about to run down the main stairs to the ground floor when they heard the *boing boing boing* of a bed being bounced on. Then came the *smash* and *clatter* of something like a vase of flowers being thrown against a wall.

They stopped and listened outside the door of Mr and Mrs Milkwarm's room which was the nicest room in Creakie Hall.

'That's great,' said a thin, metallic voice. It sounded like the sort of voice a cockroach might have if it had a voice. 'You're smart kids, you know that?'

Boing! Boing! Boing!

Smash! Clatter! Smash!

Then came a poisonous, whining voice that Polly had already heard. It was Bruce Milkwarm. 'We know a good deal when we see one, Mrs Clawback,' he said with a nasty laugh.

Rip! Scrape! There was a sound of splintering wood.

'And it's our kind of fun,' sneered another voice. It was Taffeta Milkwarm. 'We wreck the joint and you pay us. We like strangers like you.'

'Of course you do,' replied the metallic voice. 'Just remember one thing. The job's gotta be finished tonight.'

Behind the door came the sound of gushing water.

'They're going to flood the floor,' cried Polly in a hoarse whisper. 'They're going to wreck the whole place! I've got to stop them!'

'If those Clawbacks find out we know their plans, we'll never catch them red-handed,' George said. 'We have to wait for Marmaduke and Miasma.'

'You're right,' muttered Polly miserably. 'I just hope they know what they're doing.'

George put his hand on her shoulder. 'Trust them,' he said. 'They love Creakie Hall. They'd never do anything reckless.'

'Polly! George!'

Aunt Gardenia was standing in the front hall. She looked pink and pleased with herself. Beside her stood Marmaduke and Miasma.

Polly and George walked slowly

down the stairs, unable to stop staring at the sight in front of them. Marmaduke was dressed in a magician's hat with a swirling black cloak lined in scarlet satin.

Miasma had hidden her orange hair underneath a headdress of peacock feathers and silver sequins. She was dressed from head to foot in a sparkling blue suit that glittered at the cuffs and collar with flashing rhinestones.

'It's unbelievable!' cried Aunt Gardenia. 'Just when I was asking myself what Creakie Hall could provide for those lovely children, Bruce and Taffeta, these wonderful people arrived on my doorstep.'

'We're entertainers,' chuckled Marmaduke, winking at Polly and George. He lifted his hat and six white rabbits flew onto the chandelier.

Polly's face went grey.

'Goodness,' cried Aunt Gardenia. 'Magicians are so clever these days.'

There was a dull *thud* behind them. Osbert Codseye sank in a heap on the floor.

'Poor Osbert,' laughed Aunt Gardenia. 'He had a terrible turn in the garden. He said a bullfrog flew past his ear.'

'Oh dear,' said Miasma with a big grin on her face. 'That must have been *terrible*.'

'Last time he had a turn, I knitted him his very own cosy cover,' said Aunt Gardenia, sweetly. She picked up her knitting needles. 'This time I think he needs a body bag.'

And with that she dragged Osbert Codseye into the dining room and shut the door gently behind her.

'Excuse me,' said a small, frightened

voice. It was coming from behind a huge potted fern by the front of the hall. Alice Milkwarm peered out, her pale face twitching nervously. 'I was wondering if anyone had seen –'

'Dear Bruce and dear, dear, Taffeta,' cried Marmaduke in his most charming voice. He opened his gloved hand and offered her a huge bunch of red bulrushes.

'It's just that we don't know where they are,' whispered Mrs Milkwarm, clutching the bulrushes. 'And Douglas, Mr Milkwarm that is, and I, rather worry when we don't know where they are.'

'Your worries are over, Mrs Milkwarm,' cried Marmaduke, waving his other hand and presenting her with a beautifully woven basket,

covered in a snowy white napkin. 'Might I suggest that you take a stroll through the maze. A light picnic is provided.'

Mrs Milkwarm took the basket in a trembling hand. 'That's very nice of you,' she said hesitantly. 'But about Bruce and Taffeta –'

'They are playing happily upstairs,' boomed Marmaduke. 'They've made friends with our other guests, you know.'

'Such a nice young couple,' added Miasma.

'That's strange,' murmured Mrs Milkwarm. 'Bruce and Taffeta don't usually make friends. Not with nice people, anyway.'

'The strangest things happen at Creakie Hall,' replied Miasma, grinning wolfishly.

Marmaduke strode to the front

door and held it open. 'Enjoy your picnic,' he cried. 'You will find the maze, how shall I say, wholly captivating.'

Polly's eyes nearly popped out of her face. 'But the maze is like a –'

'Marvel of nature,' cried Miasma, gaily. 'It has to be experienced to be appreciated.'

Mrs Milkwarm's knuckles were white where she clutched the handle of the picnic basket. 'Thank you,' she whispered. 'You don't know what this means to Douglas, Mr Milkwarm that is, and I.'

And without looking back, she rushed down the front steps, grabbed Douglas Milkwarm's sleeve and the pair of them disappeared into the maze.

'Perfect,' said Miasma, rubbing her hands.

At that moment, Aunt Gardenia appeared at the door. A long, grey, knitted body bag grew from the flashing needles in her hands. She beamed at Polly and George. 'Such wonderful news,' she cried. 'I completely forgot to tell you. That lovely couple, the Clawbacks, well, it's all happened much sooner than I expected –'

For the first time in his life, George interrupted Aunt Gardenia. 'What do you mean *happened*?' he asked slowly.

For a moment, Aunt Gardenia looked puzzled. Then she laughed her silvery laugh. 'So many exciting things to do for Creakie Hall, they said, let's get started. So I signed and we start tomorrow.'

Polly went white, clutched the side of the table and sank onto a chair. George stood frozen like a statue.

They both thought the same thing.
It's too late.

'How exciting!' cried Miasma, giving Marmaduke a meaningful look. 'I think we shall get started too!'

'A brilliant idea,' cried Marmaduke, beaming at Aunt Gardenia.

'Why, thank you!' replied Aunt Gardenia, and she disappeared back into the dining room.

'It's all over,' wailed Polly.

'It's just beginning,' cried Miasma.

Marmaduke flashed a wide white smile at Polly and George. 'Come along, children,' he said. 'It's time we entertained our charming guests.'

Miasma took Polly by the arm and lifted her gently from the chair.

Marmaduke put his hand on George's shoulder. 'And this time,' he said with a low chuckle. 'We shall make it a family affair.'

CHAPTER 6

'DID YOU SHOW her the money?' snapped Ritzi Clawback as she outlined her thin lips in blood-red lipstick in front of the mirror.

'Of course I did, you idiot,' snarled Roger. 'Did you get those brats organised?'

Ritzi Clawback laughed a nasty laugh. 'They took to it like ducks to water,' she said.

Roger Clawback slammed the door behind him and flipped open the black suitcase. Inside there were five rows of banknotes. Each row was made up of six neat piles of money. Or at least that's what Aunt Gardenia thought. Which was exactly what she was supposed to think. In fact, only one of the piles was all money. The others had one note on top and the rest of the pile were slips of paper.

Roger Clawback picked up the pile that was all money and flipped through it, just like he had done in

Aunt Gardenia's dining room. 'It worked a treat,' he said smugly.

Ritzi yawned and smothered a smile. 'So when do we put her out of her misery?'

Roger pushed Ritzi from in front of the mirror and grinned at his own reflection. Then he reached into his pocket and held out a small piece of paper.

It was a cheque with Aunt Gardenia's signature on the bottom.

'Any time you like,' he replied. 'This dump's as good as ours now. The old bat's given us every penny she's got.'

There was a soft knock and the door began to open.

'Who's there?' shouted Roger, quickly shutting the suitcase with his foot and stuffing the cheque back in his pocket.

'Room Service,' said a cheery voice.

Miasma and Polly were dressed in crisp black uniforms. Each wore a white frilly cap and apron. Miasma was pushing a trolley. 'Caviar!' cried Polly, holding up a bowl of tiny, black, wobbly eggs.

'Champagne,' shouted Miasma, waving a large bottle of purple-coloured liquid. 'With just a hint of black cockroa –'

'Currant,' said Polly quickly. 'Compliments of Miss Gardenia.'

Miasma expertly pulled the cork and turned to pour the fizzy liquid into two tulip-shaped glasses. As she poured, she hummed a peculiar little song that went something like *Plinkity! Plink! Plink! Plonk!*

It sounded just like the noise the tiny white pills made as Miasma dropped them into the glasses.

'Chin chin! Down the hatch!

Bottoms Up! Bung ho!' cried Miasma, holding out the sparkling drinks.

If there was one thing that neither Ritzi or Roger could resist it was caviar and champagne.

Roger grabbed the fullest glass and poured it down his throat. Then he passed the other one to Ritzi. With their free hands they scooped up a dollop of caviar and dropped it straight into their mouths.

'It's the very best quality,' said Miasma. 'Russian Bullfrogia.'

'Beluga,' corrected Polly. 'Russian *Beluga*. It's the best you can get.'

'I know caviar when I taste it, dumb brain,' snarled Roger.

Miasma filled up his glass again. 'Of course, you do, Mr Clawback,' she murmured, humming her little tune. 'And it's so much nicer than frogspawn, isn't it?'

Polly's mouth dropped.

Roger stared at Miasma as he tipped the fizzy drink down his throat. 'You think I'm stupid, don't you?' he shouted. Suddenly he looked most peculiar. His cheeks went bright red and his eyes began to spin in his head. 'You think I'm nothing but a jumped-up swimming-pool attendant, don't you?'

Roger's face froze.

Ritzi's face froze.

Roger rubbed his eyes and stared at Ritzi.

'What's going on?' he muttered. 'Every time I open my mouth, something horrible comes out.'

'What do you mean, "something horrible"?' said Ritzi in a hoarse whisper. Her face had gone as white as a candle and the glass shook in her hand.

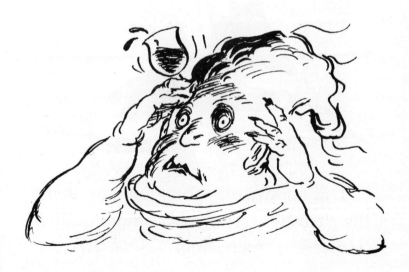

Roger's eyes bulged. 'Every time I open my mouth, he croaked, 'I have to tell the Tru – ugh! ugh! ugh!' He clutched at his throat. 'The Tru – ech! ugh! aaargh!' He sank to the floor. 'I have to tell the Truth,' he spluttered.

'Did you say you had to tell the truth?' cried Miasma, gaily. 'How very interesting.'

Ritzi Clawback's glass dropped from her hand and shattered on the floor. Not because of what Roger had said but because of what she saw in the mirror. A pair of black feelers had sprouted from her head. Two shiny black wings were folded across her back. Her arms and legs had turned into three pairs of thin, prickly legs. They ended in ridiculously long painted red nails.

Polly stared at her open-mouthed. Then she remembered something Miasma had said in the attic.

And the woman looks like a great big cockroach.

Which was exactly what Ritzi Clawback had become!

'Why have you turned her into a cockroach?' whispered Polly.

Miasma grinned. 'Because cockroaches are disgusting,' she said.

'What's more they carry nasty things everywhere they go.' She paused. 'But there is one useful thing about them.'

'What's that?' asked Polly, staring at the huge Ritzi-sized insect that scuttled about the room.

'They have lots of extra arms and legs for holding hammers and nails and screwdrivers.' She turned and glared at Ritzi with her bright-green eyes. 'TO FIX EVERYTHING THAT'S BEEN BROKEN.'

All the while Roger Clawback had been rolling about on the floor clutching his throat and gagging. Suddenly, he stood up and, as if he was in a trance, he picked up the big black suitcase and walked out the door.

Ritzi Clawback clumped after him clutching legfuls of hammers, nails and screwdrivers.

Miasma winked at Polly and the two of them pushed the trolley out of the room and shut the door behind them.

Chapter 7

ALICE MILKWARM WAS sitting next to her husband on a patch of soft grass in the middle of the maze. In one hand she held a tulip-shaped glass of clear sparkling champagne. In the other was the most delicious biscuit in the shape of a frog. She nibbled a second little leg and lay back in a pool of sunlight.

'It's most extraordinary,' she said. 'But I do think there is something magical about this place.'

Douglas Milkwarm smiled and sipped at his glass. 'There's certainly

something magical about being on our own,' he said, dreamily.

'Funny you should say that, dear,' murmured Alice. She sipped at her own glass. 'Because I have just had the most amazing idea.'

'So have I,' said Douglas Milkwarm, his eyes bright for the first time in many years. 'What's yours?'

'It's about the children,' said Alice Milkwarm, shyly.

'So's mine,' cried her husband. 'And I don't know why I haven't thought of it before.'

Alice Milkwarm sat up and took her husband's hand. 'We'll send Bruce and Taffeta to summer camp,' she cried.

'And for the first time ever,' shouted her husband, 'we won't take no for an answer!'

With that Mr and Mrs Milkwarm joined hands and danced round and round the middle of the maze until they were all dizzy. Then they fell down in the soft grass and lay about laughing.

From behind the hedge George smiled to himself. Everything was happening exactly as Marmaduke said it would.

He turned and, without making a noise, he retraced his steps and ran back to Creakie Hall.

'Holy smoke!' cried Marmaduke in his heartiest voice. 'You two *are* having fun, aren't you?'

Bruce and Taffeta Milkwarm looked up. They had just climbed the stairs to the second floor and were working their way through the first bedroom.

Taffeta had unravelled the knitted bedspread and was criss-crossing the room, wrapping the wool round all the furniture.

Bruce was standing in the middle of an upturned flower arrangement and was smearing soap over a full-length mirror.

'Buzz off,' snarled Bruce. 'We're here on business.'

'So am I, dear boy, so am I,' cried Marmaduke. 'I'm here to entertain you both.'

'We don't need no entertaining,' said Taffeta. 'As soon as we're finished here, we're leaving this dump.'

Marmaduke threw up his hands in mock surprise. 'But what about your dear parents?' he asked. 'It's their holiday too.'

Bruce Milkwarm turned and stuck out his chest. 'Can't ya read?' he muttered. 'It says *KIDS FIRST*. And that's the way it is in our family. We do what we want.'

'Yeah,' said his sister as she cut a pair of heavy silk curtains in half. 'And we don't take no for an answer.'

'Quite right,' cried Marmaduke. He sat down on what was left of the bed. 'But after all this hard work, aren't you getting a little bit hungry?'

'What if we are?' said Bruce. As he spoke his stomach rumbled. 'We'll steal something from the kitchen.'

'Oh, don't do that,' said Marmaduke, jumping up. 'Allow me to save you the trouble.' He swept his shiny black cloak through the air and revealed a trolley covered in hamburgers, chips, hot dogs, chocolate, ice cream and soft drinks.

Bruce and Taffeta couldn't resist it. Without a word of thank you, they fell on the food and gobbled it up like pigs.

Which is exactly what they turned into.

You could tell which one was Taffeta because her black and white snout was smeared in chocolate.

Bruce on the other hand had become large, pink and bristly.

'Hey!' cried his sister. 'You're a pig!'

Bruce whirled round and glared at her with pink piggy eyes. 'You're a pig yourself,' he grunted.

'Don't you call me a pig,' screamed Taffeta. At that moment, she caught sight of her reflection in the mirror. 'Bruce,' she croaked. 'Look in the mirror!'

Bruce turned and found himself staring at a drooling pig wearing a

KIDS FIRST T-shirt.

He gasped. Then he gulped. Then he lay down and began to howl. **'I WANT MY MUMMY!'**

'I WANT MY DADDY!' squealed Taffeta and great piggy tears rolled down her face.

They looked around the room and for the first time they saw what a mess they had made. And it wasn't just this room. They had already wrecked the others on the first floor. Even worse, they realised how mean and horrible they had been to their parents. How they had behaved like pigs all their lives.

Marmaduke said nothing. He just stood staring at them with his strange black eyes. As if by magic, Bruce and Taffeta decided they would go to summer camp so their parents could enjoy a holiday on their own.

Then they started to sob louder than ever. For the first time in their lives, Bruce and Taffeta were sorry.

'What on earth is going on?' cried George as he opened the door. 'What are these two pigs doing in here?'

Marmaduke twirled a gloved hand. Mops, buckets, brushes, sponges and an invisible mending kit appeared. 'They're cleaning up all the mess they made,' said Marmaduke, looking sternly at the two pigs snuffling in the corner.

'But what about everything that's been broken?' asked George. 'I've just looked in the other rooms and –'

There was a scratch at the door.

'Come in,' said George. Then he nearly fell over. A huge black cockroach clumped into the room.

Hanging from its neck was a bag of nails. Tucked just inside its broad shiny back wings was every kind of hammer, chisel, screwdriver and saw. But the strangest thing about this cockroach was its legs. They ended in ridiculously long painted red nails.

'Ah, Mrs Clawback!' cried Marmaduke. 'You've spoken to my wife, I see. And what of dear Roger?'

Ritzi Clawback waggled her antennae miserably. 'He's gone to see Miss Gardenia,' she said in a thin, metallic voice. 'He said he had to tell her the truth.'

'Excellent!' cried Marmaduke. Then he fixed the pigs and the cockroach with his fierce black eyes. 'You will leave Creakie Hall as you found it. You will clean and repair absolutely everything.'

The pigs picked up mops and buckets. The cockroach laid out her tools. Marmaduke ushered George out of the room and shut the door behind him.

CHAPTER 8

MR AND MRS MILKWARM walked slowly back across the lawn to the front door of Creakie Hall. The sun was setting and their faces glowed in its red-gold rays.

But their faces would have glowed anyway, because Mr and Mrs Milkwarm had changed completely. Their heads were held high. Their eyes were shining. And their minds were made up.

Aunt Gardenia was sitting on the front doorstep. Beside her was a huge pile of unpicked black and purple wool and a tulip-shaped glass of sparkling wine. In her hands were the last few rows of a black and purple scarf. The sun glinted on her spectacles as her eyes wandered to the two people walking towards her. Who on earth could they be? Aunt Gardenia put down the black and purple scarf. Unravelling wool always made her confused. But just recently, it seemed to Aunt Gardenia, things had been rather confusing anyway.

First, Roger Clawback had appeared in the dining room and told her he was terribly sorry, that he was a swimming-pool attendant, really, and could he at least teach Osbert Codseye to swim to make up for the trouble he'd caused.

Then just as Aunt Gardenia had finished knitting Osbert a pair of swimming trunks, Osbert had hidden in the middle of a rosebush, and refused to come out. Then Roger had said sorry again, paid his bill in cash and left a suitcase full of white paper behind him. Aunt Gardenia was sure she had seen the suitcase before. She took another sip of the delicious wine the man in the cloak had brought her. The trouble was she couldn't

quite remember. It was as if a whole lot of things had just disappeared from her mind.

And as for Ritzi Clawback, that was another puzzle. While Roger was waiting in the car, she had knocked on Aunt Gardenia's door, told her that Creakie Hall was the loveliest place in the world, that it had made her a different person and that Aunt Gardenia shouldn't ever change a thing about it. At the time Aunt Gardenia had been so surprised all she could do was stare at Ritzi Clawback's ridiculously long red painted fingernails. They were all chipped and broken.

Aunt Gardenia smiled to herself and pulled apart the last few rows of the black and purple scarf. Come to think of it, she couldn't remember why she had knitted the scarf in the first place. She never did like black and purple together.

'Excuse me,' said Mrs Milkwarm. 'Douglas and I would like to tell you that we think Creakie Hall is absolutely *magical*.'

Aunt Gardenia laughed. It was a high tinkling sound just like a silver bell. 'I'm so glad you like it,' she said. 'We think it's magical, too.'

'We certainly do,' said Polly, sitting down beside her.

'The strangest things happen *all the time*,' agreed George.

'Have you seen Bruce and Taffeta?' asked Douglas Milkwarm.

Polly nodded. 'They're packing their bags upstairs.'

'They're *what*?' gasped Mr and Mrs Milkwarm.

At that moment Bruce and Taffeta came down the main stairs and into the front hall. They looked completely different. Their faces were clean. Taffeta's hair was brushed. And Bruce was wearing a brand new T-shirt. It said, *PARENT POWER*.

'We had this great idea,' explained Bruce. 'We thought we would like to go to summer camp and then you can have a lovely holiday here.'

'And we won't take no for an answer,' said Taffeta, sweetly.

Mr and Mrs Milkwarm couldn't believe their eyes. They knew things had changed. But they thought it was just them. Mrs Milkwarm put her hand on her children's foreheads. 'Are you sure you are feeling well, dears?'

'Never felt better,' said Bruce, smiling. He lifted up the suitcases. 'If we leave now, you can be back at Creakie Hall by supper time.'

In the middle of a rosebush Osbert Codseye looked up. Something horribly familiar was flying round and round Creakie Hall. It looked like a heron with black curly head feathers and a sword tied round its middle. Sitting on its back was a huge black bullfrog. Its head was thrown back and Osbert could have sworn he heard it laughing.

Osbert Codseye groaned and slumped to the ground. Maybe he wasn't taking enough exercise. Maybe he should learn to swim, after all.

Aunt Gardenia stood on the front steps and watched as Mr and Mrs Milkwarm left to take Bruce and Taffeta to camp. 'Such charming children,' she murmured. 'Didn't I say so when I first saw them?'

'What happened to Marmaduke and Miasma?' asked George.

'Who?' said Aunt Gardenia.

'The, um, entertainers, you introduced us to,' said Polly.

'Ah, yes,' replied Aunt Gardenia. 'They had to go.' She shrugged. 'Something about a cardcastle.'

From the dining room came the muffled sound of a cuckoo inside a cosy knitted cover. 'Gracious!' said Aunt Gardenia. 'Is that the time? I must see to Osbert.'

Polly and George stood alone in the front hall. The portraits of Miasma and Marmaduke Bogey-Mandeville over the fireplace seemed bigger than ever.

Polly stared up at them. 'George!' she whispered. 'Look!'

Instead of a book in his hand, Marmaduke was stroking a large white rabbit. Beside him, Miasma cuddled a shiny black bullfrog!

ABOUT THE AUTHOR

Karen Wallace was born in Canada and spent her childhood messing about on the river in the backwoods of Quebec. Now she lives in Herefordshire with her husband, the author Sam Llewellyn.

For more information about *The Ghosts of Creakie Hall* series and other Catnip books visit

www.catnippublishing.co.uk